PRE

D0997852

FAIRY TALE MIX-UPS

The Elves
Help
Puss In Boots

written by Paul Harrison
illustrated by Tim Sutcliffe

Essex County Council

3013021225513 6

Once upon a time, there was a cat named Puss In Boots. His master, Jack, fell in love with a princess. Puss defeated an **ogre** so Jack could have the ogre's castle. Then Jack married the princess.

Everyone was very happy. Everyone except Puss. His wonderful boots were worn out. They needed mending.

4

Puss went to
the **cobbler** in the
nearest town.

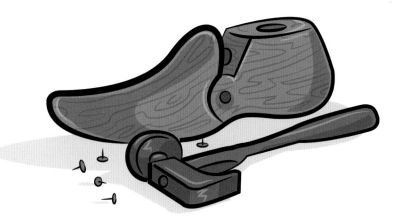

"Can you mend
my wonderful boots?" he asked

"They are wonderful boots, but I'm
afraid I can't fix them," the cobbler
replied. "They are too small and fine for
my big hands."

Puss went to the next town and the next, but the **cobblers** always told him the same thing.

Finally one cobbler said, "Boots that wonderful must have been made by fairy folk. I hear that there's a shoemaker in the next town who has elves working for him."

Puss ran to the town as *fast* as his legs would carry him. When he arrived, he stopped *in front* of the shoemaker's shop. He couldn't believe how lovely the shoes in the window were. He walked inside and showed his boots to the shoemaker.

"Ah, *fairy boots!*" he said. "Yes, I can *fix* them. Come back tonight and you can watch."

That night, Puss returned to the shoemaker's shop. Puss and the shoemaker hid in a cupboard so the elves wouldn't see them. They peered through the gap in the door and waited.

As the clock struck **midnight**, two elves appeared dressed in rags.

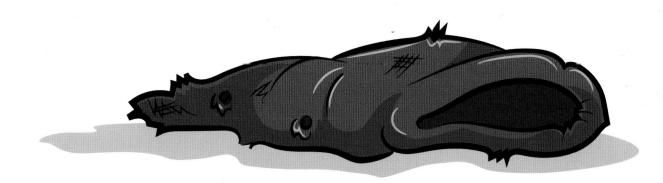

Puss watched as the elves worked.
In no time at all, his boots were
mended. Then the elves disappeared
into the night. The boots looked as
good as new – better even!

Puss was overjoyed.
But the shoemaker
was not.

"What's the matter?" asked Puss.

"I want to **reward** the elves," said the shoemaker. "But they have no use for money. I thought I might make them new clothes instead. I can't find a thread that is strong yet fine enough to use."

It was true. The elves deserved something for all their hard work. Puss thought long and hard. Where could they find thread that would do the job?

He scratched his whiskers. That was it! His whiskers would work perfectly!

Puss plucked out a couple of whiskers and gave them to the shoemaker. The shoemaker went to work straight away.

That night they set out the new clothes for the elves. Then they both waited *for* the clock to strike **midnight**.

When the elves saw the clothes, they jumped around the room with joy. Puss had saved the day!

Puss In Boots

The *Puss In Boots* story that is well known was written by French writer Charles Perrault in 1697. In this story, Puss belongs to a miller's son. The miller's son is poor, but Puss is clever. Puss catches rabbits and other animals to give to the king. The cat pretends they are gifts from his master, who Puss says is a rich young man. Puss then defeats an **ogre** so the miller's son can live in the ogre's castle. The king is impressed with the gifts and the castle. The miller's son marries the king's daughter.

The Elves and the Shoemaker

This story comes from two German brothers called Jacob and Wilhelm Grimm. They collected fairy tales from Europe during the 1800s. In this story, a poor shoemaker has only one piece of leather left to make shoes. He goes to bed and wakes to find that elves have turned the leather into a pair of beautiful shoes. The elves, who are dressed in rags, come back each night to make more shoes. The shoemaker becomes rich. To thank the elves, he makes them some new clothes. The elves are overjoyed.

Glossary

cobbler – someone who mends shoes

midnight – twelve o'clock at night

ogre – a monster or giant who eats people

reward – give a gift or award for doing something good

Writing prompts

Write a thank-you letter from the elves to the shoemaker. What do you think they liked most about their new clothes?

Can you retell the story from the cobbler's point of view? How pleased do you think he was when Puss came up with his great idea?

Imagine you were hiding in the cupboard with Puss and the shoemaker. Describe what it would be like waiting for the elves to come. What could you see at midnight?

Read more

Puss in Boots (My Classic Stories), Nina Filipek
(Milly&Flynn, 2013)
Puss in Boots (Read it yourself with Ladybird), (Ladybird, 2015)
The Elves and the Shoemaker (Read it yourself with Ladybird),
(Ladybird, 2013)
The Elves and the Shoemaker (Well-loved Tales), Vera Southgate
(Ladybird, 2015)

Websites

www.grimmfairytales.com
Read and hear fairy tales by the Brothers Grimm on this
website. They wrote the first *Elves and the Shoemaker* story.

**www.hellokids.com/r_51/reading-and-learning/tales-for-chil-
dren/classic-tales/charles-perrault-tales**
Charles Perrault wrote the well-known *Puss In Boots* story. Read
more of his stories on this website.

www.kidsgen.com/stories/folk_tales
Read lots of different folklore stories from different cultures on
this website.

Read all the books in the series:

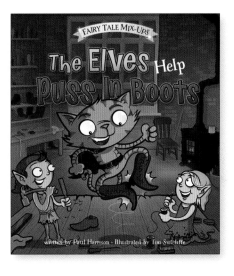

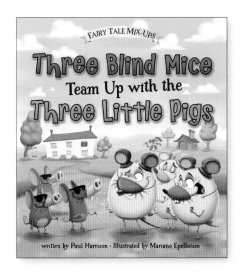

Visit www.raintree.co.uk

Raintree is an imprint of Capstone Global Library Limited, a company incorporated in England and Wales having its registered office at 264 Banbury Road, Oxford, OX2 7DY – Registered company number: 6695582

www.raintree.co.uk
myorders@raintree.co.uk

Text © Capstone Global Library Limited 2017
The moral rights of the proprietor have been asserted.

All rights reserved. No part of this publication may be reproduced in any form or by any means (including photocopying or storing it in any medium by electronic means and whether or not transiently or incidentally to some other use of this publication) without the written permission of the copyright owner, except in accordance with the provisions of the Copyright, Designs and Patents Act 1988 or under the terms of a licence issued by the Copyright Licensing Agency, Saffron House, 6–10 Kirby Street, London EC1N 8TS (www.cla.co.uk). Applications for the copyright owner's written permission should be addressed to the publisher.

Edited by Penny West
Designed by Steve Mead
Original illustrations © Capstone Global Library Ltd 2016
Illustrated by Tim Sutcliffe, Inky Illustration Agency
Production by Steve Walker
Originated by Capstone Global Library Limited
Printed and bound in China

ISBN 978 1 474 72755 6
20 19 18 17 16
10 9 8 7 6 5 4 3 2 1

British Library Cataloguing in Publication Data
A full catalogue record for this book is available from the British Library.

Every effort has been made to contact copyright holders of material reproduced in this book. Any omissions will be rectified in subsequent printings if notice is given to the publisher.

All the Internet addresses (URLs) given in this book were valid at the time of going to press. However, due to the dynamic nature of the Internet, some addresses may have changed, or sites may have changed or ceased to exist since publication. While the author and publisher regret any inconvenience this may cause readers, no responsibility for any such changes can be accepted by either the author or the publisher.